J E C
Catalanotto, Peter.
More of Monkey & Robot

W9-BAZ-042

Norfolk Public Library

MORE OF MONKEY & ROBOT

Also by Peter Catalanotto

MORE OF
MONKEY
& ROBOT

by
PETER CATALANOTTO

A Richard Jackson Book

ATHENEUM BOOKS FOR YOUNG READERS
New York London Toronto Sydney New Delhi

To DJ—for the best of friendship

*Thank you, Lauren Rille and Ariel Colletti,
for your talent and patience!*

𝒜
atheneum

ATHENEUM BOOKS FOR YOUNG READERS

An imprint of Simon & Schuster Children's Publishing Division • 1230 Avenue of the Americas, New York, New York 10020

This book is a work of fiction. Any references to historical events, real people, or real places are used fictitiously. Other names, characters, places, and events are products of the author's imagination, and any resemblance to actual events or places or persons, living or dead, is entirely coincidental.

Copyright © 2014 by Peter Catalanotto

All rights reserved, including the right of reproduction in whole or in part in any form.

ATHENEUM BOOKS FOR YOUNG READERS is a registered trademark of Simon & Schuster, Inc.

Atheneum logo is a registered trademark of Simon & Schuster, Inc.

For information about special discounts for bulk purchases, please contact Simon & Schuster Special Sales at 1-866-506-1949 or business@simonandschuster.com.

The Simon & Schuster Speakers Bureau can bring authors to your live event. For more information or to book an event, contact the Simon & Schuster Speakers Bureau at 1-866-248-3049 or visit our website at www.simonspeakers.com.

Book design by Lauren Rille

The text for this book is set in Adobe Jensen.

The illustrations for this book are rendered in graphite pencil and ink.

Manufactured in China

1213 SCP

First Edition

10 9 8 7 6 5 4 3 2 1

Library of Congress Cataloging-in-Publication Data

Catalanotto, Peter.

More of Monkey & Robot / Peter Catalanotto. — 1st ed.

p. cm

"A Richard Jackson Book."

Summary: Presents four stories about best friends Monkey and Robot, who try out Halloween costumes, visit the beach, consider what to do with a tire they find, and figure out if it is morning or night.

ISBN 978-1-4424-5251-0 (hardcover)

ISBN 978-1-4424-5253-4 (eBook)

[1. Best friends—Fiction. 2. Friendship—Fiction. 3. Monkeys—Fiction. 4. Robots—Fiction.] I. Title. II. Title: More of Monkey and Robot.

PZ7.C26878Mor 2014

[E]—dc23

2012051501

CONTENTS

Who IS Who?

"What are you thinking about?" Robot asked.

"I'm thinking about what I'm going to be for Halloween," Monkey said.

"But it's only June," Robot said. "Halloween is four months away!"

"I know," Monkey said, "but I messed up last Halloween."

"Well," Robot said, "most people don't like it when you stick your fingers in their mouths."

"I was a dentist!" Monkey protested.

"I know," Robot said, "but real dentists wash their hands and wear gloves before they touch someone's teeth."

"I should have worn my mittens," Monkey said.

"Do you want to be something scary?" Robot asked.

"No," Monkey said. "I want to be something that everybody likes."

There was a knock at the door. Robot opened it. Mrs. Harper was standing there with a big plate of cookies.

"These are for you," Mrs. Harper said, "because you fed my cat last week while I was away."

"It was my pleasure," Robot said. "Would you like a cookie with a cup of tea?"

"Oh yes!" Monkey said. "But I would like my tea in a big glass with lots of milk and no tea."

"I was asking Mrs. Harper," Robot said.

"I can't," Mrs. Harper replied. "I need to take Snowflake to the vet."

"Is something wrong with Snowflake?" Robot asked.

"No," Mrs. Harper said. "She's just having her teeth cleaned."

"I'm glad," Robot said.

"Why are you glad?" Monkey asked. "Does Snowflake have bad breath?"

"No," Robot said. "I'm glad that nothing is wrong."

"Thank you," Mrs. Harper said. "You're always so nice." She turned and hurried down the walk. Robot closed the door.

"I've got it!" Monkey shouted. "I'm going to be you for Halloween!"

Monkey ran to his bedroom. Robot put the plate of cookies on the kitchen table.

When Monkey came into the kitchen, he was holding a sheet of blue paper, scissors, a belt, and a roll of tape. Monkey cut out a triangle from the paper and taped it to his shirt. Then he took a pot out of a cabinet and put it on his head. "Now I am you!" he said.

"What is the belt for?" Robot asked.

"Turn around," Monkey said.

Robot turned around, and Monkey taped the belt to Robot's bottom. "Now you are me!" Monkey said.

Robot looked at himself in the hall mirror. "But I don't look like you," he said.

"Well," Monkey said. "You will have to act like me too."

"Are you going to act like me?" Robot asked.

"Of course! Watch." Monkey walked around the room without bending his arms or legs. "And I'm going to use big words and say smart things, like the word 'photograph' starts and ends with the number *F*!"

Robot just stared.

"Now you act like me," Monkey said.

"The word 'photograph' starts with the letter *P* and ends with the letter *H*," Robot said.

"Perfect!" Monkey shouted. "Keep saying funny things like that!"

"But, Monkey . . . ," Robot said.

"Come on," Monkey said. "Let's see if the neighbors know what we are."

Mrs. Harper was at the vet, so they knocked on Mr. Walker's door. Mr. Walker peeked at them through his window and asked, "What do you want?"

"We want to ask you a question," Monkey said.

"Are you going to stick your fingers in my mouth again?" Mr. Walker asked.

"No," Monkey said.

Mr. Walker opened the door.

"What are we?" Monkey asked.

"Is this a joke?" Mr. Walker asked in return.

"No," Robot said.

"You are a monkey and a robot," Mr. Walker said.

"Hooray!" Monkey yelled. "It worked!" He ran home.

"Thank you, Mr. Walker," Robot said.

When Robot got home, Monkey was sitting on the couch. He looked very sad.

"What's the matter, Monkey?" Robot asked.

"My birthday is next month," Monkey said. "If everyone thinks I'm you, I won't get cake or presents."

"Just go back to being you," Robot said.

Monkey jumped up. He took the triangle off his shirt. He took the pot off his head. He took the belt off Robot's bottom.

"Am I me again?" Monkey asked.

"Yes," Robot said.

"We should make sure," Monkey said. He grabbed Robot's hand and pulled him back to Mr. Walker's house. Monkey knocked on the door.

Mr. Walker opened it and asked, "Now what?"

"What are we?" Monkey asked.

"A pain in the neck," Mr. Walker said.

"Please," Robot said. "If you tell him what we are, we won't bother you again."

Mr. Walker sighed. "You are a monkey and a robot," he said.

"Hooray! I'm me!" Monkey cried. He started skipping home.

"Thank you, Mr. Walker," Robot said.

"Is your friend always like that?" Mr. Walker asked.

Robot looked at Monkey skipping home. He smiled.

"Yes," Robot said. "Yes, he is."

At the Beach

"Let's go in the water!" Monkey said. "I love swimming!"

"I want to," Robot said, "but I would sink and then I would rust. But you may go swimming if you'd like."

Monkey looked at the ocean. He was so hot, and the water looked so cool and refreshing. But he didn't want to swim if Robot couldn't.

"No," Monkey said. "I don't really like swimming."

"But you just said you love to swim," Robot said.

"I used to," Monkey said. "But not anymore."

"Would you like to build a sand castle?" Robot asked.

"Sure," Monkey said.

Monkey and Robot walked to the edge of the water where the sand was wet and perfect for building a castle. They used their shovels to fill their pails. They dumped pail after pail of the wet sand into a huge pile.

"This will be the greatest sand castle ever," Robot said.

"Yes," Monkey said. He liked building the sand castle with Robot, but he really wanted to jump into the water. Monkey felt sweaty and itchy. There was sand in his bathing suit.

"Are you sure you don't want to go swimming?" Robot asked.

"I'm sure," Monkey said.

Robot knew Monkey wanted to go into the water. He knew Monkey felt sweaty and itchy. So when Monkey was busy filling his pail, Robot buried his shovel in the sand.

"Oh no!" Robot cried. "My shovel is missing."

Monkey looked around. He did not see Robot's shovel.

"Maybe a seagull picked it up and then flew away," Monkey said.

"There are no seagulls around here," Robot said. "They are all by the garbage container."

"Maybe the wind blew it away," Monkey said.

"The wind is not strong today," Robot said.

"Maybe a dog picked it up and then ran off," Monkey said.

"There are no dogs on this beach," Robot said. "There is a sign that says No Dogs Allowed."

"Maybe it was a dog who cannot read," Monkey said.

"No," Robot said. "I'm afraid my shovel might be in the water."

Monkey jumped up. "I'll save it!" he shouted. Monkey ran into the water and started to splash around.

"I don't see your shovel!" Monkey yelled.

"Maybe you should swim on your stomach and look for it," Robot yelled back.

"Good idea!" Monkey said. He swam on his stomach, but he did not see the shovel.

"Maybe you should swim on your back and look for it!" Robot called out.

"Good idea!" Monkey said. He swam on his back, but he did not see the shovel.

"Maybe you should do the dog paddle and look for it!" Robot yelled.

"Good idea!" Monkey said. He did the dog paddle, but he did not see the shovel.

"Maybe you should look under the water," Robot yelled.

"Good idea!" Monkey said. He dove under the water. Monkey popped his head up and said, "I don't see your shovel under the water."

"Please keep looking," Robot yelled.

"Don't worry," Monkey said. "I will find your shovel." Monkey dove under the water again and again.

After Monkey dove under the water ten times, Robot dug up his shovel and then waved it in the air. "I found it!" he shouted.

Monkey came out of the water. He felt cool and refreshed.

"Where was it?" Monkey asked.

"It was buried in the sand," Robot said.

"Oh," Monkey said. "I'm glad you found it."
He dried his face with his towel.

"Thank you for looking in the water for my shovel," Robot said.

"It was my pleasure," Monkey said. "I would do anything for you."

"I know," Robot said. "Let's finish our sand castle."

Robot and Monkey made the greatest sand castle ever.

The Tire Swing

"Why is there a tire in the house?" Robot asked.

"I found it in the front yard this morning. Then I planted an acorn," said Monkey.

Robot blinked three times.

"Acorns are seeds that grow up to be oak trees," Monkey explained.

Robot waited.

"I'm going to tie this tire on a branch of the oak tree, so we can have a swing," Monkey said.

"Ah," Robot said.

"Will you help me?" Monkey asked.

"Of course I will help you." Robot picked up a book and then sat on the couch. He started to read.

"I thought you were going to help me," Monkey said.

"I will," Robot said.

"Then let's go," Monkey said.

Robot put down his book. "Your tree won't be ready for a long time."

"Tomorrow?" Monkey asked.

"Longer," Robot said.

"Next week?"

"Much longer," Robot said.

"A month?"

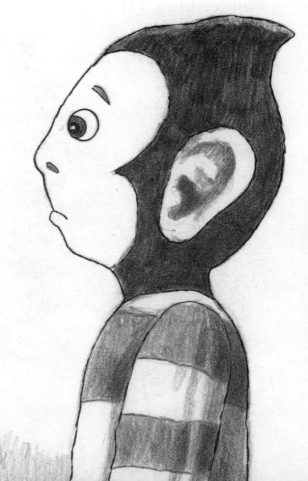

Robot shook his head.

"A year?" Monkey asked.

"Your grandchildren will be the first ones to swing on that tire when it hangs from your oak tree," Robot said.

"Wow!" Monkey said. "I'll go tell them the wonderful news!"

He ran out the door.

Robot didn't get up to close the door.

He knew Monkey would be right back. A minute later Monkey returned. "I don't have grandchildren," he said.

Robot nodded.

"When will I have grandchildren?" Monkey asked.

"When you have children," Robot said, "and when your children have children, then *those* children will be your grandchildren."

Monkey closed his eyes and quietly repeated what Robot said. "That's a really long time," Monkey said.

"Yes, it is," Robot said. Monkey sighed.

"This tire might belong to someone," Robot said.

"Hmm," Monkey said. "Perhaps we should hang pictures of it all over town, so whoever lost it will know we found it."

"Good idea," Robot said.

Robot and Monkey sat at the kitchen table and drew lots of pictures of the tire.

Robot picked up a roll of tape. "Let's go," he said.

"Should we bring the tire with us?" Monkey asked.

"Yes," Robot said. "It will be fun to roll the tire as we walk."

Robot and Monkey walked to the end of their street with the tire and the drawings.

"Should we go up the hill or down the hill?" Monkey asked.

"The owner of the tire probably lives up the hill, because I think the tire rolled down the hill to our house," Robot said.

"It will be really easy to roll the tire down the hill," Monkey said. "Watch."

Monkey pushed the tire with one finger, and it started to roll by itself.

"Run after it!" Robot yelled.

Monkey and Robot
chased the tire down the hill.
They ran as fast as they could. The tire rolled
faster and faster. It hit the curb, flew through the
air, and bounced off an oak tree.

"Run away from the tire!" Robot shouted.

Monkey and Robot turned and ran. The tire landed in front of them. They both tripped over it and fell down.

While they were lying on the grass, panting, a girl ran up to them. "You found my tire!" she said. "Now I can make my swing!"

Monkey sat up. "Do you have grand-children?" he asked.

"No," the girl said.

"If you live here, how did this tire get up the hill to our house?" Robot asked.

"I don't live here. I live way up the hill. I was playing with the tire, and it rolled away from me."

"You should be more careful," Monkey said.

Robot looked at Monkey.

"My grandfather lives here," the girl said. "He planted this tree a long time ago. We're going to make a swing."

Robot and Monkey stood up.

"Thank you so much for bringing my tire to me," said the girl. "Would you like to play on the swing when it's ready?"

"Yes!" Monkey shouted.

"We would love to. Thank you," Robot said. He gave her the drawings of the tire. "You may keep these in case you ever lose your tire again."

"Someday you can come to our house and play on our swing with my grandchildren," Monkey said. "But I have to have children first."

"Ah, okay," the girl said. She waved good-bye and rolled the tire toward her grandfather's house.

"Let's go home," Robot said. He started up the hill.

"Hey, guess what?" Monkey asked.

"What?" Robot asked.

"I'm tired," Monkey said. "Get it?"

"Very funny," Robot said.

Eight O'Clock

"What time is it?" Monkey asked.

"It's eight o'clock," Robot said.

"Is it eight o'clock in the morning or eight o'clock at night?" Monkey asked.

"That's easy to figure out," Robot said. "What do you do at eight o'clock in the morning?"

"I eat breakfast," Monkey said.

"Correct," Robot said. "And what do you do at eight o'clock at night?"

"I go to bed," Monkey said.

"Correct," Robot said. "So, are you hungry or are you sleepy?"

"I'm hungry," Monkey said. "So it must be eight o'clock in the morning."

"It must be," Robot said. He put on an apron. "I'll make breakfast."

"But what if it's eight o'clock at night and I am asleep and I am dreaming that I am hungry?" Monkey asked.

"Oh my," Robot said. "I never thought of that. Well, dreams often have odd things happen in them. Do you see anything that is odd?"

"Yes," Monkey said. "You are wearing a dress."

"This is an apron," Robot said. "I wear it so I do not get food on myself when I make breakfast."

"Oh," Monkey said. "Then everything looks normal."

"Good," Robot said. "What would you like for breakfast?"

"I want toast with peanut butter and banana. I want cereal and milk. And I want apple juice," Monkey said. He rubbed his tummy.

"What's the magic word?" Robot asked.

"Abracadabra!" Monkey yelled.

"No," Robot said. "You need to say 'please.'"

"Abracadabra, *please!*" Monkey yelled.

"You just need to say 'please,'" Robot said. "'Please' is the magic word."

"Oh," Monkey said. "May I *please* have toast with peanut butter and banana, and cereal and milk? And may I *please* have apple juice?"

"Of course you may," Robot said.

Robot went into the kitchen. Monkey set the table.

"Oh dear, we're out of bread," Robot said. "Please go next door and ask Mrs. Harper if we may borrow two slices of bread."

Monkey put on his boots and his sweater. He went next door and borrowed two slices of bread. He returned home, took off his boots and his sweater, and said, "Here is the bread!"

"Oh my," Robot said. "The peanut butter jar is empty. Please go next door and ask Mrs. Harper if we may borrow a spoonful of peanut butter."

Monkey put on his boots and his sweater and went next door. He came back, took off his boots and his sweater, and said, "Here is the peanut butter!"

"Oh no," Robot said. "We don't have any bananas!"

Monkey went next door and borrowed a banana.

"No cereal!" Robot said.

Monkey went next door and borrowed a bowl of cereal.

"The milk carton is empty!" Robot said.

Monkey went next door and borrowed a cup of milk.

When Monkey returned, Robot was standing in the kitchen, holding an empty jar of apple juice. Monkey sighed. He put on his sweater and his boots and went back next door and borrowed a glass of apple juice.

"Perfect!" Robot said. "Now go sit at the table, and your breakfast will be ready soon."

Robot made breakfast and put it on a tray. He carried it to the table. Monkey was not sitting at the table. Robot looked in the living room. Monkey was not there, either.

"Monkey!" Robot yelled. "Where are you?"

"I'm in bed," Monkey said.

Robot went into Monkey's bedroom. "I thought you were hungry," he said.

"I was," Monkey said. "But that was when I thought it was eight o'clock in the morning. Now I know it must be eight o'clock at night, because I'm very sleepy."

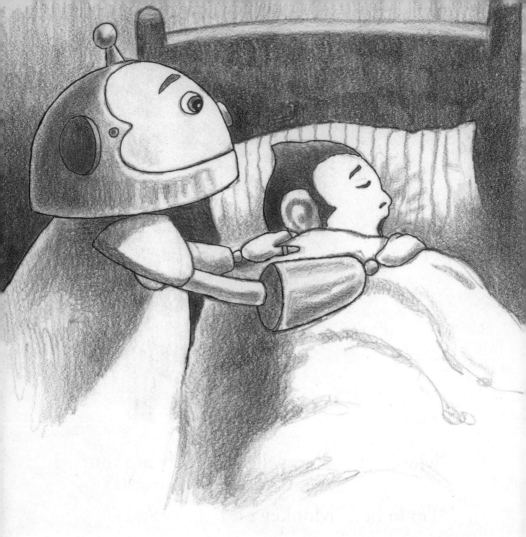

Robot tucked the blanket snugly around Monkey. Then he pulled the window shades down.

"Sleep well," Robot whispered.

Monkey snored softly.